Short Relief

Ben Shahon

.406 Press

ISBN 978-1-967135-02-8

Book Cover by Scott Bolohan

.406 Press | Troy, MI
www.406press.com

Contents

Rub Some Dirt on It

"I TELL YOU, I just want to punch that kid in his fucking head. Look what he did to you. Who just lets their kid swing a bat without telling him to hold on?"

Your father asks you this while holding a wrapped-up paper towel under your broken nose in the bathroom at the public park. It's the rough kind of paper towel, the kind that sucks up a lot of fluid but feels awful to the touch. The skin under your nose is soft, and wet, and the paper towel feels like you're face down on a boulder. Ordinarily that wouldn't bother you so much—you like sitting on top of boulders, after all—but with your father jamming your head toward the sky, just trying to stop the bleeding, something about it feels wrong. You feel the blood rush down the back of your sinuses, and into your throat.

"Dad," you say, his hand hurriedly readjusting your uniform, "what good would that do?"

Your father sighs, and shakes his head in the way you've seen many times before. It's the same shake he gives when he knows you're right, that he knows he doesn't have a way to come back from what you've just said, but still feels enraged that you are in pain. You try to look strong for him, to pretend that a broken nose doesn't bother you, and say that you'll go back out there and play the rest of the game, no hard feelings. Eventually the bleeding stops, and you make your way to the field in time for out number three. You're still on deck, and the umpire looks at you, blood staining the lettering on your jersey. He points back to the coach standing next to the pitching machine within his little white circle, more a part of the field than on it. Your mom wanted to take pictures today; she still has the camera dangling around her neck when you flash her a smile of red teeth. Your coach, his hand still bloody from holding your nose, signals back to the plate.

The ump yells, "Play Ball!"

Throwin' Slop

JULIUS STEVENS (#34, B-L, T-L) stands on his hill, and he turns his head to his left, then to the right. He's got the lowest ERA of anyone in the Pacific Coast League, and that's not about to change right now. A pair of runners at first and third, top of the second, one out on the scoreboard, and the popcorn vendor shouting about the snacks he's trying his hardest to push. A horn blares, screaming its presence at an unblinking blue sky. There's no wind over the ballpark today—which Stevens wishes would at least pick up to a small breeze, since the knuckleball dances better that way. It isn't really worth throwing anyways, most days, but it would at least give him something to set up the fastball with.

The runner at first dives back to the base before Stevens even finishes turning his shoulder to make the pickoff throw. Stevens pulls the hat off his head, wipes his brow, and puts his glove up to get the throw back from Arthur Wallace (#13, B-S, T-L) at first. The two have been friends since Wallace had been called up to the San Marcos Shakes from AA back in March. Stevens had been around since about '54 or so, and the manager Harry Hartson (#82) assigned the two to room together on a long road trip. Wallace thought he was going to get called up any day now, which gave Stevens quite the chuckle in the clubhouse.

"I don't even need a locker here, guys," Wallace would say, packing his street clothes into a bag, conveniently hidden in the back corner of the clubhouse, behind the laundry basket full of sweaty, used towels. "But I'll be sure to reserve seats for you guys in October."

"Seats for what? Your community theater performances?" the left fielder, Jimmy Fish (#5, B-R, T-R) would chide, holding up his glove like an opera mask.

"C'mon, Jim. His performance isn't even up to that level." Reliever Max Klein'd (#22, B-L, T-R) always know how to clear a room. It makes Stevens worry that he's going to be called in to clear the bases now.

Stevens looks back down the barrel of the battery at his catcher for the day, Morris Poe (#76, B-R, T-R). He shakes off the sign for all the off-speed pitches he knows: curveball, change, knuckle, and slider. What he's looking for, the fastball low and away, is just not coming out of Poe. Figures. Backups never quite seem to know the game plan as well as the regular starters do. But they eventually get it through their thick skulls.

Nodding at the fastball call, Stevens gears up to throw. It isn't quite as easy as it used to be when he first started; his joints have started to firm up with arthritis, he has strained every muscle and broken all three bones in his arm, and his ankle always seems to click when he pivots on it now. But Stevens still knows how to huck the ball across the plate. He has to, since almost all of his other pitches are basically the same batting practice slop at this point. A better pitcher would have worked on refining his craft, tried to build longevity for his final few years trying to make it all the way up to the show. Stevens is not that pitcher. At 34, he is on the older side of the fireballers, but he still insists on trying to wear out his arm as fast as possible, at least, according to Hartson. He likes it better that way. It keeps him feeling young, for a bit longer.

The ball seems to exit the strike zone much quicker than it entered it. Stevens looks up in awe as it flies across the sky, dangerously close to the right field foul pole. Luckily for him, it lands to the right of it.

Poe yells something back at Stevens, probably asking if he's done trying to do Poe's job for him, but Stevens doesn't care. He catches the throw from Poe with his body turned toward the runner at first. The runner dances back and forth next to the bag, and Stevens simply puts his hand and glove on either hip, cocking his head disappointedly at Wallace, who is looking up at his fiancé in the nosebleeds, ignoring the runner taunting him and Stevens.

"Hey dickhead! You wanna play ball sometime today?"

Wallace snaps back into focus, and hustles the five feet separating him from the bag. Being a lefty, Wallace throws up his right hand, covered by the most worn out glove on the team. Hartson has wanted him to get a new one, but Wallace insists that the bruising on his fingers was worth the comfort of knowing that the glove would make the play. He isn't going to chance it on a new one, even if he has to tape his fingers up before and after every game.

Stevens drops his right foot back to the rubber, looks back and forth at the runners, cocks his left leg up over his waist—higher than usual for him—and drops his foot to the first base side. Wallace is ready, and receives the throw that no one had signaled for.

"Balk!"

Hartson flies out of the dugout, frothing at the mouth like a rabid dog. He yells every obscenity he knows at the umpire, who stoically ignores him, and signals for the play to continue. The players look around at each other, confused, as the runners advance, and Wallace dishes the ball back to Stevens. He pitches a third strike, sending the crowd into a minor fervor. The next batter, Jeremy Dubner (#52, B-R, T-R), enters his designated box. Dubner played with San Marcos last year, and Stevens would often room with him on the extended road trips. A smart aleck, Dubner spent a lot of his free time doodling, making wild cartoons out of the twisted faces and misshapen bodies you would find walking around with the club. They are quite the cast of freaks; at least that's what Stevens thinks. Which, probably, is why he and Dubner got along in the first place.

Still trying to yell the umpire's ear off, Hartson starts to run out of breath as Dubner gets set in the box. "Let it go, Harry," Stevens yells down. "It's really not worth it."

"Yeah, coach," Dubner chimes in, "it's just one runner on base."

Hartson keeps shouting that the umpire needs to just open one of his shit eyes, since he's got two of them in his fucking head anyways. He finally gets tossed, and storms back to the dugout in a huff.

Dubner and Stevens laugh it off, and settle back into the usual routine.

"Going to try and strike me out now, Stevens?"

"I'm not going to try to strike you out. I'm going to strike you out. Period. End of story."

"Good luck. I've been taking extra batting practice for this series."

"Lotta good it'll do ya."

"For sure. For sure."

Stevens gets the sign for a 12-6 curve, which makes him laugh. His curve now probably only goes from about ten to eight by now. Or is it two to four? Does it even really matter?

He shakes the sign off, which makes Poe call time. Blue grants it, and Poe drops his mask to the ground, and starts marching up the bump to Stevens. Lot of good it'll do him.

Wallace starts tapping his foot like he does when he wants the ball. Everyone knows that this isn't going to be a short visit. Stevens catches a glimpse of him out of the corner of his eye, nodding toward first so that the umpire can see. The ump nods back, and Stevens tosses the ball to Wallace. He catches it with the glee of a puppy fetching one from the yard, throwing it back and forth with his fellow infielders, third baseman Bob Sands (#46, B-R, T-R), shortstop Edgar Diaz (#15, B-L, T-R), and second baseman Rick Griffin (#2, B-R, T-R). Stevens looks back to Poe, who is taking his sweet time marching to him. His breath is short, as though the short walk was enough to get his heart beating a bit. How someone so unathletic could have made it this far boggles Stevens' mind.

"What the hell are you doing out here, Stevens?"

"I'm pitching."

Poe isn't satisfied.

"Seriously. Do you want to get shelled today?"

"No. I want to throw. So, get back behind the dish."

"Then listen to what I call."

Stevens spits saliva to the ground, as he shifts his chew from one cheek to the other. This fat kid doesn't know what's good for him.

"I'll throw what I know how to throw."

"Do you not know the other pitches?"

"I don't know how to throw shit pitches, if that's what you're askin.'"

Poe rolls his shoulders and inhales. After looking for a moment like he's going to sneeze, he pushes the air painfully through his nostrils. Furrowing his brow and shaking his head, he says,

"Fine. Fine."

As Poe walks back—torturously slowly—to the catcher's box, Dubner shouts back, "Can I be invited to the tea party next time, guys? Please?"

Stevens chuckles as he settles back into his motion. Time for the next pitch. Poe starts to cycle again, until Stevens finds the fastball that he wants. He nods, confirming Poe's suspicion that he's only going to throw one pitch for the rest of the afternoon. It's a chilly, April day, and despite the lack of wind, the sun hasn't poked through the overcast, coastal sky.

Dubner hits the ball down the line. It rolls to first, spiking up on a pothole in the grass, and bouncing high over Wallace's head. He takes a few steps back, and fields the ball on the hop. Stevens sprints to first, putting his glove up to his shoulder, awaiting Wallace's throw.

However, the first baseman instead decides to try to beat the runner and the pitcher to the bag himself. The three men crash together, falling over and dropping the ball. Dubner snaps back first, seeing another defender coming to grab the ball and tag him out, and dives to first base.

Stevens wakes back up in the clubhouse, with a bag of ice tied to his head, and a transistor radio at his feet.

"Well, Fran, I don't know about you, but I sure hope that Julius Stevens can make it back alright for the next game.

"Yeah, Mark. It would be a real shame for him to miss out on what looks to be a good season coming up for the Shakes."

"It sure would. We're going to have to take a commercial break now. At the end of four, it's Shakes 1, Bees 5."

Stevens clicks off the radio. This isn't his game anymore, so there's no use worrying about what his teammates are gonna do. They can take care of themselves. He digs around in his locker for a clean towel, the one he brings back and forth from his apartment during homestands, and places it folded on the bench by the showers.

Looking in the mirror, Stevens unwraps the ice bag from around his forehead. The bump is pretty good, but he'll be fine. It looks like he crashed skulls with Dubner out there. It's probably going to hurt like a motherfucker when he gets under the hot water.

It does.

Stevens cleans up, and wraps the towel around his waist. He grabs his razor from the locker, since now is as good a time as any to clean up his shave. If the boys win tonight, they'll want to go out, and Stevens wants to look sharp. It's been a few years since he and Marsha split, and it's probably for the best. She wanted kids, and from what Stevens has heard, she finally got them.

The cold razor blade almost immediately draws blood from Steven's cheek. The blood slithers down his face, but he chooses not to wipe it, instead focusing on finishing his cheeks, chin, and neck before those animals get back inside the clubhouse. Their hooting and hollering are not conducive to having a blade to your neck. Stevens splashes the hot water on the cut, watching it close up and stop bleeding. He looks at his mustache intently in the mirror, and spots three gray hairs, which he immediately plucks.

Stevens gets dressed and exits the clubhouse. He decides that if he isn't going to play in the game anymore today, he might as well try sneaking upstairs like a casual fan. It's minor league ball, so it isn't likely that anyone out here is going to recognize him, especially with his sunglasses on and no hat. Well, anyone except for Dubner.

"So, you're trying to sneak out too?"

Stevens turns around, and finds himself face-to-face with his ex-teammate.

"I thought it might be fun to play hooky and catch the ballgame today. You?"

Dubner laughs, responding, "Thought I might try to see some friends while I'm in town. I hear Marsha's doing pretty well."

"One day, I'll have to really lay into you with that mouth of yours."

"You'll never catch me. Hell, you can't even throw one that could catch me."

"The fastball was working fine today."

"If you call that batting practice slop a fastball."

Stevens windmills his right arm forward.

"That's right, kid. Stretch it out, else, you might get sore."

"Funny."

"I know," Dubner says. "That's why I said it…Anyways, I gotta go. See ya 'round, bud."

"See you."

With that, Dubner leaves the facility. Stevens moseys over to left field—the deep seats never sell out on a day like today—and finds a suitable spot near the back. He looks out to the scoreboard in right field. The boards tell him that the current score is Bees 6, Shakes 3, in the bottom of the ninth, two outs.

Wallace steps up to the plate. Stevens expects the curveball, since Wallace can't really hit it all that well. Wallace looks fastball, taking a huge cut and missing. The next pitch is a changeup that scratches the dirt. 1-1. Fireball, up and in, almost takes off Wallace's head. He doesn't really need to be hit there again today. Hitter's count, Wallace needs another fastball. Stevens sees the slider coming, though. You can just tell by how he's standing on the mound.

Wallace grounds out up the middle, 6-3.

Out

WHEN THE BAT CRACKS, I get a text from you, telling me to go home with one of the boys, because the key to our apartment won't work if I go back there, and that I'll need to call you when I want to come by and pick up my stuff, that you're kicking me out, because you found the emails on my computer and you know about Lena, and the time she came over when you were out of town, the time she and I had agreed instantly was a mistake, and had agreed never to speak of again, to delete every last shred of evidence for, except for this one I secretly kept out of a misplaced sense of sentimentality, to leave on that fateful night in what was at the time our apartment, but which I suppose is now your apartment, even though I found the damned place, this damn email which had a picture of the two of us, Lena and I, wrapped in one another, kept as a memory, because as much

as neither of us cared to admit it that night or any time since,

I had fun, and I still think of her from time to time, even as I

sit here watching grown men play a game like a bunch of

scared little boys, sitting from hundreds of yards away, but

still a hell of a lot closer than I've felt toward you in a long

time.

Buy Me Some Peanuts

SOMETIMES THERE IS NOTHING BUT RAGE IN YOUR GUT, and you don't know what to do but hit something. So, you get in your old brown pickup truck—the kind that gets seven miles to the gallon—and drive way out to the batting cage on the edge of town. You can't swing a bat as well as you used to, but there's still some force when you manage to put your hips into it. You line up at the fifty-mile-per-hour cage, right behind all the old, fat slow-pitch guys that want just to show off to one another that they still got it. But before long you start to realize the error of your ways, and walk down to the eighty and ninety-mile-per-hour cages, the ones where there is no reasonable expectation for you to be able to hit the ball.

You plop your quarters into the little receptacle like you're getting ready to play some old video game. The beer league guys wander over to watch, expecting you to look like they do in their fifties.

The first pitch comes hard and fast, and your swing less so. You were so confident that you thought you could just take your time warming up. The old farts start laughing at you, begging you to stop. You don't. You take another hack, and it looks like it would have gone far, save for the net. And you hit another. And another. The old guys stop laughing, their smug grins turning to something akin to shock, fear. They've never seen an animal like you before. They tell themselves they're going to go home at the end, and give their old balls and chains a piece of their mind, even if in actuality they're just going to collapse in their lazy boys, drunk off their fat asses. It doesn't matter, they weren't the ones who got fired today. And the fire in your gut starts to bubble over, and out into your outstretched wrists. And the balls start to fly. And before long, you don't remember why you were here in the first place. And before long, you don't remember why you were here in the first place. And before long, you don't remember why you were here in the first place.

On Deck

STEVENS SAUNTERS OVER TO HIS CAR, the last one in the lot, a beat-up little coup. Some Italian piece of garbage that he bought ten years ago, when he thought it would be any day now until he got called up, and would need to show up at the fields looking like hot shit for the fans. Now, it's just some car that's too small to help a teammate move in, to take the guys out for a drink, or even to really sit comfortably in alone. Stevens wants desperately for the keys to stop working one day, for it to get switched with some other guy's car, and have him go along with the trade.

It's a small fantasy, but that's the kind that gets him through days like today.

He winds down Interstate 15, a newer highway built by the Eisenhower administration. Got to respect a military man's devotion to a good road. Not that Stevens ever gave much of a shit about fighting the good fight; he just needed the road to get into town to see Marsha. He passes orchard upon orchard of avocado trees, their near-ripe fruit ready to pop, fall over, and expose the green and black inside.

Marsha isn't expecting Stevens to show up today, and why would she? It isn't like he called and said that he was coming down to see her today, or checked in with her husband to see if it would be alright to disrupt their dinner plans with a midday highball. That was something Stevens always liked about Marsha; no fucking around with some girly drink. Straight to the beer or the cheap stuff for her. Hell, maybe with a little less of it they would have made it.

He cuts the engine and stares at the window. Marsha's kitchen faces the street, and he can see her pulling the dough from the mixer, rolling it out and cutting strips to place in a casserole dish. Stevens taught her to do that. He always liked the casserole to have a real kind of flair to it, the kind of thing that would befit a man of his station. She turns away from the half-cut dough in a panic, scrambling, until she grabs a pot lid from the sink and turns to the stove.

Barely shutting the car door behind him, Stevens jogs up to the door. He runs his fingers through his hair, one last time, and raps his fingers twice on the frame. The screen swings open toward him in the spring breeze, but he pushes the door shut as he awaits a response.

"I'm sorry, but now's not a great time! I just spilled my pot pie all over my apron!"

Stevens thinks about opening the door up, coming straight in, and offering to help her with the dinner. He figures that he'd probably start by taking her apron off of her, running his hand slowly down her back, and untying it with one hand. He'd find her rags, mop up what was surely spreading all over the floor by this point, and start rinsing the rags until the gravy and vegetables were nowhere to be found. He'd call the boys in, have them set the table, making sure there were places for both Stevens and their dad, as well as the rest, and then have dinner with Marsha and Paul, the accountant. But he doesn't.

Then he has a much worse thought. Or a better one. No, worse. He thought he could just wander in, take off her apron as before, and start to lick the pot pie filling, piping hot from just coming off the stove. He would suck it all down, then he would move on to Marsha herself. He would drink her as heartily as he consumed the pot pie filling, and Marsha would sit there and take it. He knows deep down that there's no way in hell that he could pull off this kind of move—least of all with a married woman—but there's still some part of him that holds on to it. He thinks he hears Marsha call out, "Jules?"

Feeling guilty about the last horrible thought that he had, Stevens starts to figure what's the right thing to do. He thinks about walking in, telling her, "I'm sorry for barging…"

"What are you doing here?"

"I'm here to say that I'm sorry."

"About what?"

"I'm sorry that I took too long. That I'm still taking too long. That I couldn't give you this life. I know that this is what you wanted, and I think I wanted it, too. I'm sorry that I couldn't be a good father for these boys, that I couldn't leave the game. It's just that—"

"Jules, I'm not sure that I really have time for you today. Can you come back tomorrow?"

Then, Julius would look up at the blue sky behind him, and stop and think a bit more. He would consider what it would really take to give it all up now, leave it all behind. The team doesn't really need him. He's the best starting pitcher on a AAA team from San Marcos, not the goddamn Yankees, after all. Then the fantasy starts to fade, and he realizes, "I can't. I have to be getting back, actually. It was good seeing you Marsha, and I really, truly am sorry."

But Stevens doesn't have this conversation either. He just grumbles, "Sorry to disturb you ma'am. Thank you for your time," in a voice that isn't his own, and turns back to his toy car.

Stevens doesn't notice in his rear-view mirror that Marsha comes out to look and see who was at the door, turning her head up and down the street, before going back inside to clean up the mess she made. Instead, he just drives away until he reaches downtown San Diego, where his teammates are waiting on him.

"What took you so long?" Diaz asks.

"Nothing. I just needed to stop at home for a minute."

"Why?"

Stevens huffs, "I had to give my housekeeper's ass a good tongue polish," he says ruffling his 'stache. "Shit. 'S my bad. I really shouldn't talk about your mom like that."

Diaz looks away, like he always does when Stevens talks about women, shaking his head in disgust. Stevens doesn't give a shit, though. He made himself laugh, and that was the real point.

Stevens, Diaz, and the others abandon the sunset for the swank of the nightclub. Wallace pushes his way to the front, fat steak tied to his forehead, and a nice shiner on his face. "I thought I was the one to get hit in the head today," Stevens dishes. Wallace laughs it off and heads straight to the stage. Since the proposal, he's acted like a goody two shoes, since his fiancée is real strict about him chasing skirt. This is the closest he can get. Stevens finds it tragic.

Stevens files into a booth with Diaz, Fish, Klein and Poe. He can't believe that the guys invited that fat fuck to come with them, but here he is, sucking wind and drooling all over his dumb chin. Wondering if Poe's already sloshed, Stevens grabs a rolling paper from his jacket, rolls it up, and tries to land it in Poe's gaping jaw. It bounces off, and Diaz asks, "So, are you just trying to fuck with all of us tonight? What's the fucking deal, vet?"

Looking up to the stage sheepishly, Stevens ignores the question. No one wants to be called a AAA vet. As far as he's concerned, he's still a prospect, just waiting for the call. Can't think of it any other way, else they'll never call you up. At least, that's what his pops used to tell him.

Wallace comes back and sits on the other end of the booth with Fish and Klein. Stevens can hear the two of them talking about how they made the atom bomb, how they stuck it to those Axis-holes, and how the U.S. would totally drop another one if those Russian commie bastards got too big for their britches. Stevens feels a little bad for Wallace, since the kid was born in the war, he hadn't known his old man, lost on the ground doing special ops when the bombs hit in Hiroshima and Nagasaki. He would step in and change the subject, but Poe and Diaz have him pretty locked down over on this end.

Excusing himself to get a drink, Stevens gets up and goes to the bar. He orders a whiskey, and waits for the bartender to find something for him in the back. He twiddles with a Babe card that he keeps in his wallet. It was one that he bought right before he got drafted. He always thought it would be cool to play with the Bambino, or even against him, or shit, just have a beer with the guy. Everyone knows that he likes to have a good time. Stevens pulls out a cigarette, and right after lighting it, he hears a voice ask, "Got any more matches, sug?"

Reaching into his loose shirt pocket for the one item that he can find of value on him, he pulls out a match and lights the cigarette, watching the flame burn down off of the edge of stick, until it hits the smoothed edges of his fingertips, which the young blonde girl wearing a spiralingly multi-colored tank top would have expected to be rougher, until Stevens explains that he makes sure after every game to wash them in this special soap that he remembers that his mom used to make to use for herself, since her hands were always rough after working in the kitchen and the garden all day, which makes the girl blush, seeing as she is little more than a girl after all, but Stevens feels alright talking to her, seeing as she has to be old enough to get into this club without getting carded and ordered a drink without anyone batting an eye, not even those idiots in the corner who look closer in age to her, too busy jerking each other off about the recap of the Shakes game from earlier that day to notice that a nice chick is sitting right here, if Stevens could even call her nice, considering all of the dirt and grime that she has under her fingernails and on her sandaled toes, making Stevens wonder if this is one of those new hippie chicks that he keeps hearing about from the guys, since they all seem to think that hippie chicks will do whatever you tell them, so long as they weren't more interested in fucking each other than you, which Stevens has heard about once or twice, but he'd have to see it to believe it, seeing as he had never met a girl that he couldn't sleep with, except of course for Marsha, and the thought of her almost brings him back to tears, even though Stevens is a man dammit, and men don't cry in public, that's what women do, and this little chick has no reason to cry, no reason to take on all of his baggage, not when she's pulling out her cigarette from her mouth and putting it in Stevens's maw, pushing it in his face so fast that he nearly burns his whiskers trying to make the transition from one to the other, and the smoke pulses through his lungs, deeper than the chick thinks that he should inhale, but Stevens keeps going, taking a good long puff, before falling out of his chair to the floor, much to the delight of the girl, who thinks it's adorable to see a big strong man such as himself reduced to a crumpling pile of meat and bones for her, until she offers her hands to Stevens, helping him up, and he notices that her fingers are far, far rougher than his, almost to the point where he wonders aloud if she's the pitcher instead of him, and yeah, she played softball at one point, pretty competitively too, but it isn't like anyone really gives a shit about women's professional sports, even though that's part of what she's trying to change, seeing as she has

this whole twenty step plan to make women the next

dominant group in America, at least, that's what Stevens

thinks she's talking about, since she speaks too fast and too

smart for him to be able to keep up, even when she cajoles

him for not keeping up, and Stevens makes a joke in return

about him not being as fast as he once was, pulling back to

reveal that he was really just talking about the fastball, that's

it, there's nothing else at play, nosiree, which lets the girl

laugh a little more and invite Stevens out to her bus outside,

which makes Stevens wonder if she's really just the bus

driver that was supposed to take them to Palo Alto tonight

for the game tomorrow, but is relieved to find out that she

hadn't ever heard of the town, and he follows her outside to

her Volkswagen, Stevens glimpsing from over his shoulder

his teammates giving little waves and kissy faces at him as

they walk out the front door, stopping ultimately at this

dingy green thing that Stevens would kill to drive, pointing out his little Italian car to the girl, who just laughs at the fact that such a big guy would choose to drive such a little car, even though, as she says, cars aren't really meant for driving first and foremost, laying down in the back and patting Stevens to come and join in the back, which he quickly does, pulling his shirt unbuttoned quickly and directly and pulling hers up as well, as their lips meet and he starts to pull the belts out from their loops, stopping when she asks if Stevens has a condom, which is something that he usually carries, even if there doesn't happen to be one in his wallet tonight, but he just kisses her again before she asks for a second time, and by this point they are both so ready to go that neither of them really care much for what the end is supposed to be, and they share it, one true moment of human connection, before he flops over and lays next to her for a moment, her completely asleep moments after their interaction ends, before pulling up his pants and rolling over to lie away from her, facing the coolly metallic door of the van, dreaming of

Marsha, and wishing that he didn't have to be in goddamn Palo Alto in the morning, but he manages to slip off to sleep, because by this point the moon has come up high, and the sun has descended beyond the earnest Pacific, to some other faraway place, where he doesn't have to face it again until tomorrow, even if there is some part of him that wishes tomorrow will never come.

At the Shop

"ALRIGHT THERE, SPORT, just give it a good huck."

"Aw, I dunno, Dad. What if I miss and I hit you?"

"Son, I don't know how hard you think you can throw. But I can assure you, that even if you hit--oof!"

Mikey's dad was on the ground, and Mikey had no idea what to do. He told his dad coming out here to try to pitch was a bad idea, even if his dad said he could handle it.

Mikey's dad had played some ball back in the day, and was always trying to get Mikey to play. Mikey was a big, strong kid, taller than all but two kids in his grade, but had never really liked sports. It was all too macho for him, and he didn't like the other kids acting like he was some kind of sports robot every time they had PE. He would have been much happier staying in the classroom, building an actual robot with his teacher's erector set, but she insisted he go out and exercise with the other kids. And when his friends decided to all sign up for baseball, Mikey didn't want to. But he told his parents, and his dad decided at once they would come out here and get to training.

"Dad, do you want me to bring you some ice? Or call an ambulance? Or something?"

"Don't be silly, Mikey. This is fine. I'm fine." Mikey's dad spat blood on the dirt as he stood up. Mikey looked at him with concern, but his dad smiled at him with bloodied teeth.

"Throw the next one, Ace."

Throw the Next One, Ace

WHEN PHIL WAS YOUNG, he went to the barber with his dad. He remembers the smells more than anything: the liquid they keep the scissors in and its associated pungent odor, the shampoos and their cleanliness, and the sickly-sweet candies growing overripe in the drawer below the cash register. He hated that place from the moment he set foot inside; he wanted nothing more than to run out, go back to the car, and wait for his dad to be done and come drive him home. But he knew that if he turned to run, his dad, big and strong, would simply scoop Phil up in his arm, and carry him to the red leather chair. He remembers the little block of wood they put on the seat for him, to make him tall enough for the barber to reach, and the way it felt like it was splintering his rear. He swore that day that he'd never get another haircut. He even kept it up a few years, until his dad told him that he looked like a girl, and would have to go back. Phil was far less resistant that second time, steeling himself and accepting his fate. But when he got to the barber shop, all he saw was a bunch of guys hanging around, watching a ball game on the TV, and cracking jokes. It didn't seem so scary to be there anymore. Phil felt at home waiting for a haircut. He would like the way the other guys would call his dad 'Mikey,' especially when he only ever heard his mom call him Michael or Dad, and the way they'd let him take a little candy home at the end. Phil always took the Big League Chew, since his dad would let him check it and blow huge bubbles as he hit the soft toss his dad would throw him at the park afterward. Now, he knows someday that he'd do the same for his kid, if the park hadn't been bulldozed over for a shopping center. But for now he's got to go into the shop and get cleaned up, since it's time to see his dad again, and let him know Phil's coming home.

Around the Horn

YOU SNEAK INTO HIS ROOM about an hour after he falls asleep. As you sit and watch his snoring, elevated from the odd angle he's at from resting on a glove under his pillow, you start to wonder if it was a good idea to let him sleep with the thing. He insisted that he needed to, that there would be no other way for him to get as bonded to this glove as the last one. You wanted to chastise him for being so foolish, but another feeling swept over you. This one encouraged you to let him be a little boy a bit longer, since, after all, twelve-year-olds don't stay twelve forever. You already felt like shit for losing the old glove in the first place, despite encouraging him to take more personal responsibility for his belongings. It still felt bad to let down this boy who expects you to take care of him in these little ways. You reassured yourself that it was okay because you do a good job with the big stuff, especially since your parents skipped town. You've been the best surrogate parent an older sibling could be, even bought him the new glove before the next practice so he wouldn't have to sheepishly ask to borrow one, let him pick out the most expensive one you could afford. Walked him through all his sports psychology visualizations, even though you thought it was mumbo-jumbo. You'll be there for the game tomorrow too, but for now, you'll just let the kid sleep.

Palo Alto

STEVENS GETS ON THE BUS the next morning same as everyone else. He drove the little shitty Italian car home in the middle of the night last night in order to afford himself a few hours of sleep in a plush bed, rather than the steel one of that girl's Volkswagen. He knows Hartson won't listen to any bullshit about him being stiff having pitched so little the day before, and that he can only milk the head injury for so long.

He tries to grab a spot on the bus with a little light, but not too much. Somewhere the young ones will leave him alone long enough to sink his teeth into an Edgar Rice Burroughs book.

***

When they get to their lodgings for the night, Stevens diverts from the group for a few minutes to get a pack of smokes. But the real reason he's at the convenience store is that he needs dimes.

He puts one in the slot, and waits for the ring on the other end of the receiver.

"Hello?"

"Hey Marsha. It's—"

"Jules, I recognize your voice. I'd recognize it anywhere."

Stevens knows that isn't true, but doesn't decide to push it.

"I'm…sorry about that. I was just in town and was going to visit you the other day, but got caught up with the other guys from the team. It was a tough loss and—"

"And they wanted to go out drinking?"

"Yeah."

"Well, they drink if they win or if they lose, so I guess I shouldn't be too surprised."

She was right, but Stevens didn't want to push it too much further.

"Look, I just wanted to tell you… I just wanted to say…I'm telling you…"

But as much as Stevens tried to explain to her that he had come to the house and had tried to talk to her and apologize, he just couldn't get the words out right. Instead he started talking about how they're still married, dammit, and that it isn't right for his woman to be telling him how their relationship is going to be. Because it's his house that he paid for and there should be nothing stopping him from going home and being the good dad he knows himself to be, but Marsha started talking about cops and saying that he had better stay away or she'll have her new man tell them Stevens is a trespasser. He slams the phone back on the hook, and gets back on the bus. He doesn't say another word the rest of the ride up to the motel.

***

That night, Hartson ends up needing him on the mound again in relief against Palo Alto. They've got some scrubby kid up at the dish, a little left-handed infield type. Looks like the kid must be fast; Stevens is pretty sure that a strong wind would blow the kid over. Since he's not the better pitcher he wants to be, it'll be the same as always, a steady diet of no-longer-quite-so-fastballs.

The first one blows past the kid no problem. Stevens knows that Poe's not too happy about it, but he doesn't care tonight. Tonight, he knows he's dealing.

Stevens pulls his left foot back to the rubber. He digs his toe in for leverage as he pulls his right leg up high. Stevens is a gun that fires in one direction, and lifting his leg as high as he does at his age gets him the leverage of the hammer. He finally pulls the ball from his glove as he starts to swing his right leg back forward, whipping his elbow back with a force that he just knows will snap it off his arm someday. He's already blown out that left elbow a couple of times, so it's only a matter of reps before it eventually gives for good. But tonight, filled with the anger of the conversation with Marsha, it's made of steel. He brings his momentum forward like a pile driver, ready to extend himself fully out, whipping the trebuchet of his left arm forward at last, pulling his arm faster than he ever thought it could go, or so it always seems with Stevens. He thinks about the way the top speeds for a fireballer are so close to the top speeds allowed on a highway, and how the young kids seem stronger, faster than that even. He wonders at what point the danger posed to man by an automobile are less than the dangers posed to a man by a pitcher, but his ability to control that danger has passed him by, as the ball has already left his hand hurtling toward the batter facing an 0-1 count. But the kid standing at the dish, a kid probably not even old enough to drink yet, catches a piece of it, and sends the ball sailing over the left-center field wall. Shit. That's going to cost the Shakes the ballgame. Fucking Hartson's going to be pissed.

***

Julius takes the Greyhound bus back down to San Marcos, since the Shakes don't have an allowance for getting cut players back to wherever they need to go. Julius knew something like this was going to happen someday, that there would be a time in every man's life where he could no longer play the boys' game. And as he rode back down the state, his face in his dimestore paperback, the words glossed over his eyes, because all he could think about was home. He knows there's no going back to Marsha, and that there's no use in calling the Volkswagen chick. Just because she was a bit of fun doesn't mean she'd want to spend any more time with a washed-up has-been like him. There's a part of him that thinks the only thing left to do is take the little Italian car down south, and drive

town to town until he finds a team willing to put up with

him. He knows that the Mexicans typically let older

American guys fill out the scrub spots on his rosters. The

least he can do now is participate in mop-up duty.

But there's a part of him that doesn't want that either.

A part of him that's tired, that really thinks it's time to be

done, once and for all. And he wonders that if he really came

clean to Marsha, really apologized, and really showed

himself to be a good, stable man with a job and a real interest

in his kids, if things could be different with her too. Maybe

it would be worth it even if that weren't the case.

***

Julius is standing on the mound again. It's the bottom

of the ninth, two outs, he's pitching for Chicago, and

standing at the plate is George Herman Ruth. Babe is up to

bat, and Julius can hear Governor Roosevelt rooting for him

from the stands. Julius knows the man in the stands is

beloved, will be president one day, and that he's the man opposing the future president's favorite player, the only obstacle to the Bambino's next big moment of glory. He watches Babe lift a finger, toward the sky, the cocky prick that he is, and he spits on the ground in response. This is a game that will be played on his time, and no one else's. He winds up for the first pitch, and blitzes it past Ruth like he was pitching against a kid in a sandlot. He sails another one past the Sultan of Swat before the Yankee faithful even know what's happening. The stadium draws silent, desperate for their worst fears not to be realized. But Julius is ready to play the villain for them today, since it would mean the culmination of his career to pitch a no-hitter in the Series, especially finishing off the best hitter in baseball to do it. He finally opts to switch things up, knowing the moment doesn't call for his trademark fastball, but a filthy breaking pitch, the kind they write songs about. He lets the curve rip, and watches as Babe takes the bait, reaching way out in front for the fastball he expected that never comes, crumbling to his knees and falling on his fat ass in shame. Stevens revels in the victory, even embracing that fucker Poe, who Stevens knows is an All-Star, even if he's still a piece of shit, but none of it matters in the moment because the Cubs have just beat the Yanks to win it all, become champions of the world. And that's all that really matters, in the end.

***

When the bus gets back to San Marcos, Julius shakes himself awake. He dreamt about winning it all, even though he's at the point where he knows now that can't happen. His time in the game is finally up, for good this time, and as he walks to the little Italian car, he doesn't even bother to bring the glove with him from the bus. The driver calls out after him that he forgot it, and he thanks the guy, but Julius just puts it in the trunk of the car without a second thought. It'll probably sit in there for years at this point, but it's not like Julius really cares. He drives to his shitty little apartment, sits in his recliner, and pops a beer. It's nine in the morning, but who cares. You don't have to be sober to look through the help wanted section of the newspaper, and that's his whole plan for the rest of the day.

These stories appeared in the following journals

"Rub Some Dirt on It" in *Flash Boulevard*

"Throwin' Slop" from *Free Library of the Internet Void*

"Buy Me Some Peanuts" in *Flash Boulevard*

"Throw the Next One, Ace" in *Flash Boulevard*

About the Author

Ben Shahon is the author of one previous chapbook, *A Collection for No One to Read*. His work has appeared in journals such as *Ghost Parachute, BULL*, and *Flash Boulevard*, and he serves as the founding EIC of *JAKE*. Ben lives and writes on the border of Los Angeles and Orange Counties in California, where he bemoans the Angels' decade-plus-long playoff drought.